# Gift of the Magpie

# Gift of the Magpie

by Janeen Mason

PELICAN PUBLISHING COMPANY

GRETNA 2011

*For Kevin*

*In memory of Mambo*

*With special thanks to my talented friends, Sylvia Andrews, Barbara Bottner, Jan Fehrman, Donna Gephart, Jill Nadler, Joyce Sweeney, and my sister, Penny Bessire (who can always pull a rabbit out of her hat)*

*The word "Pelican" and the depiction of a pelican are trademarks of Pelican Publishing Company, Inc., and are registered in the U.S. Patent and Trademark Office.*

ISBN: 9781589808614

Printed in Singapore
Published by Pelican Publishing Company, Inc.
1000 Burmaster Street, Gretna, Louisiana 70053

*"Bubblegum,"* Max shouted. "Watch this, Regina." He clamped his beak shut and blew so hard a bubble popped out of his nostril.

Regina didn't call out an afternoon report like the other magpies and no one noticed but her friend, Max. He wiped his beak on his wing.

"What did you find today?" he asked

"Pearly pumps," she whispered.
"What?" He couldn't hear her over the rest of the flock.

The next morning hundreds of birds peppered the quiet dawn. Max watched for Regina.

She did a funny little flap-flap-flip with her wings that turned her a tiny smidge this way and that.

There she was. Max slipped in beside her.

"Morning, Regina."

She nearly crashed into him. "Max! You scared me."

"Mind if I come along with you today?" he asked.

Regina cocked her head. "You're not going to like it," she said.

"It's not that I don't like it, Regina. I just don't get it," Max said. "What are we waiting for?"

"Promise not to tease me," Regina said. Her head bobbed as a pair of yellow galoshes squished across the sidewalk.

"I won't tease you," he said. Work boots clumped by dangling a shoelace like a fresh night crawler. Max lunged to grab it and missed.

"Just watch," she said.

"Watch what?"

"Shoes," Regina whispered.

"Shoes?" He stared at her.

A plastic doll slipper bounced in front of them and a little hand scooped it up without missing a beat.

Regina sighed.

"You could get in trouble, Regina. The flock wants to know you found food—not shoes."

"I know," she said. "But I love shoes. Please don't tell."

"We need a plan," Max said. And for the rest of the summer they searched for food in the mornings and shoes in the afternoons.

"Look, Max—*cowboy boots.*"
"Regina—*penny loafers.*"
Together they spotted fluffy bedroom slippers
and laughed until their tail feathers shook.

But during the afternoon report they only
shouted, *"Corn," "Carrots,"* and *"Cauliflower."*
Regina fell in love with a pair of blue beaded
espadrilles. Max fell in love with Regina.
He had to tell her, but how?

Max found her in front of Fancy Feet Shoes.
"Regina, I've got a surprise for you. Come with
me."
    They skirted the edge of town, flying over the
piney woods, and landed by Big Rock Creek.

Tangled in an old root was a single forgotten sandal.

"For you, Regina. Your very own shoe." Max beamed with pride.

"For me?" Her laughter bounced through the

Max scratched the rock at his feet and held his breath.

Regina wiped her eyes. "That was funny, Max. What would I *do* with a shoe?"

He smiled a crooked smile and shrugged.

Regina giggled and lifted off. She hummed a little tune as she flew away.

Max banged his head against the tree trunk. "Definitely the wrong kind of shoe. A *flip-flop?* What was I thinking?"

Max would not give up.

For the next three days he searched high and low.

Regina worried, but on the afternoon of the fourth day he returned.

The entire flock watched as Max and three of his buddies struggled high in the air with a basketball shoe.

"How's this, Regina? Better?" Max huffed when they plopped it in the treetop next to her.

The silence was deafening.

Regina backed away from the goo that slipped off the toe.

"Max," she hissed, "you're embarrassing me."

"What? No! Wait!" He hopped into the shoe. "Look, Regina, it's comfortable and homey, and there's even room for an egg or two."

But when he turned around Regina was gone. Her wings beat a zigzag across the empty sky.

"It was the biggest shoe in the whole dump," he pleaded in a whisper.

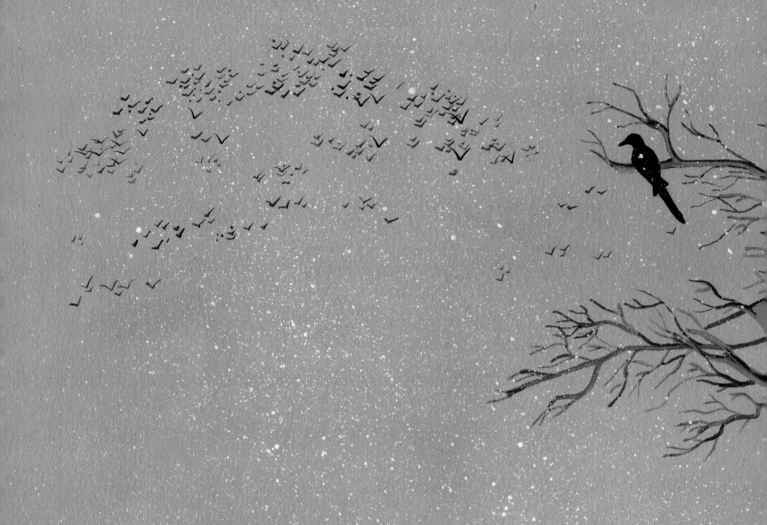

Brokenhearted, Max drifted off with the chilly winds of autumn to join another flock.

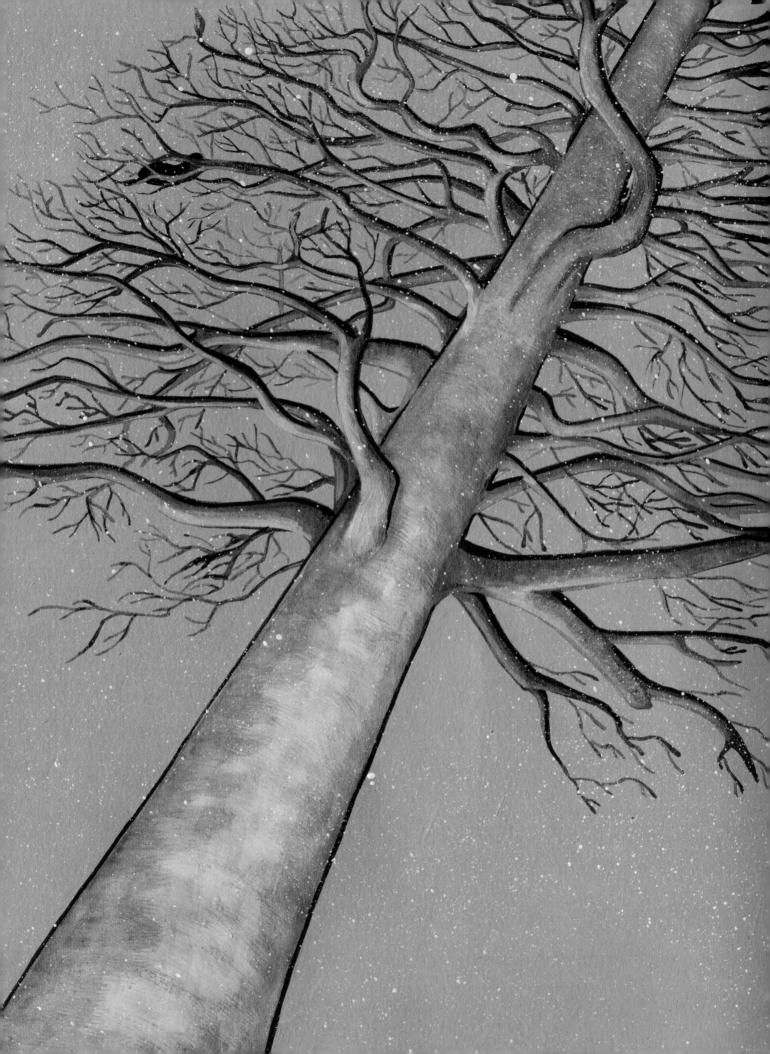

It was the grayest winter ever. Regina spied nothing but mukluks and mud puddles and frozen magpie feet.

The memory of summer made her warm inside. Up in the bare branches, she climbed into the basketball shoe and wrapped her wings around herself.

Regina was lonely.

One day she found four buttons and a string of sequins. Two days later she discovered lights left from the holidays and a little bit of lace.

Regina kept an eye trained to the sky.
On a clear afternoon, when the promise of
spring was in the air . . .

*Who's that?*

*Max.* She raced out to meet him. "You're back! Have I got a surprise for you." Regina practically knocked him out of the blue.

*"Our* very own shoe!"